CHRONICLES OF ETERNUM: UNVEILING THE ENERGY FIELD

SHANTANU AHER

Made with ♥ on the Notion Press Platform
www.notionpress.com

To those who have ever stared up at the stars and felt the pull of the unknown, this book is for you. To the dreamers, the explorers, and the adventurers, who seek to push the boundaries of what is possible and discover the secrets of the universe. To the scientists and engineers who work tirelessly to unlock the mysteries of the cosmos and bring us one step closer to the edge of eternity. This book is dedicated to you. May it inspire you to keep reaching for the stars, and may your journey lead you to places beyond your wildest imagination.

Contents

Foreword

In the vast expanse of space, there are worlds waiting to be discovered and civilizations waiting to be explored. "The Edge of Eternity" takes us on a journey beyond our wildest imaginations, where the impossible becomes possible and the unimaginable becomes real. It is a story of adventure, of discovery, and of the human spirit, a tale that will transport you to the far reaches of the universe and leave you breathless. Join us on this journey and discover the edge of eternity.

Preface

In the distant future, humanity has reached the stars and colonized countless worlds. But even in the vast expanse of the galaxy, there are secrets waiting to be uncovered. In "The Edge of Eternity," we follow Sarah, a brilliant scientist who becomes obsessed with a mysterious energy field on the desolate planet of Eternum. Her drive to uncover the truth leads her on a perilous journey through space and time, and challenges her to confront the very nature of existence. With richly drawn characters, breathtaking worldbuilding, and an intricate plot full of twists and turns, "The Edge of Eternity" is a gripping and thought-provoking science fiction epic that will transport readers to the edge of what is known and beyond.

Acknowledgements

I would like to express my heartfelt gratitude to all those who made "The Edge of Eternity" possible. To my readers, thank you for embarking on this journey with me and sharing in the wonder and excitement of exploration and discovery. To my editor, thank you for your guidance and support throughout the writing process. To the scientific community, thank you for inspiring me with your work and fueling my imagination. And finally, to the universe itself, thank you for being the canvas on which we paint our dreams. May we continue to explore the vast unknown, and discover the wonders that await us at the edge of eternity.

Prologue

Eternum, a colony on the edge of known space, had always been a place of struggle and hardship. It was a world where survival was a daily battle, and hope was a scarce commodity. But for Sarah Vega, Eternum represented something more. It was a place of discovery and exploration, a frontier where the boundaries of knowledge could be pushed to their limits.

As a young scientist, Sarah had come to Eternum to pursue her passion for uncovering the secrets of the universe. Little did she know that her work would lead her to the brink of a discovery that would change everything. In the depths of the planet's energy field, Sarah found something that no one had ever seen before: a window to the unknown, a path to the stars.

But with this discovery came a new set of challenges. As Sarah worked to unlock the secrets of the energy field and explore the uncharted worlds beyond, she would face resistance, betrayal, and danger at every turn. And as she journeyed to the edge of eternity, she would discover that the universe was far more vast and mysterious than she ever could have imagined.

CHAPTER ONE

ARRIVAL

The transport ship shuddered as it descended through the atmosphere, buffeted by high winds and sandstorms. Sarah clutched her seat tightly, trying to ignore the jolts and crashes as the ship touched down on the dusty surface of Eternum.

As she disembarked, Sarah took a deep breath of the thin, dry air, coughing as she inhaled sand and dust. She scanned the horizon, taking in the bleak, desolate landscape of the distant planet. It was nothing like the lush forests and rolling hills of her homeworld, but she had known that coming to Eternum would be a difficult challenge.

As she made her way to the colony's main settlement, Sarah was struck by the sense of isolation and hardship that seemed to permeate every aspect of life on Eternum. The few inhabitants she saw looked worn down and weary, struggling to survive in the harsh environment. But Sarah had come for a reason - she was a scientist, eager to make a breakthrough in her field, and she knew that the energy field on Eternum held the key to her success.

As she arrived at the colony's research center, Sarah was greeted by Markov, the head of the council overseeing the project. He was a tall, stern man with a curt manner, and he seemed unimpressed by her arrival.

"You're the new scientist they sent from the Academy?" he said, eying her up and down. "I hope you're ready for hard work, because life on Eternum is no picnic."

Sarah bristled at his dismissive tone but maintained her composure. "I'm more than ready for the challenge," she said firmly. "I'm here to make a difference and contribute to the research effort."

Markov grunted, his expression skeptical. "We'll see about that," he said. "In the meantime, get settled in and report to the lab in the morning. We have a lot of work to do."

Sarah watched as Markov strode away, his boots crunching on the dusty ground. She knew that earning his respect would be a challenge, but she was determined to prove herself. As she settled into her new living quarters, she looked out the window at the energy field in the distance, a shimmering, pulsating mass of light that seemed to hold the secrets of the universe.

"Challenge accepted," she murmured to herself, a gleam of determination in her eyes. "Let's see what Eternum has in store for me."

CHAPTER TWO

DISCOVERY

The air was thick with tension as Sarah made her way across the barren landscape of Eternum. The wind whipped at her face, carrying flecks of dirt and sand that stung her eyes. She felt the weight of Markov's disapproving gaze on her, and she knew that she had to tread carefully.

Sarah had always been fascinated by the energy field that surrounded Eternum, but it wasn't until she arrived at the colony that she realized the true potential of what she was looking at. As she approached the massive generator that powered the field, she felt a thrill of excitement course through her veins.

She was determined to unlock the secrets of the energy field and find out what lay beyond the shimmering veil. Markov and the council had always been resistant to the idea, seeing it as a waste of resources, but Sarah knew that there was more to the field than met the eye.

As she studied the readings from the generator, Sarah began to notice patterns that suggested the field wasn't just an energy barrier, but a wormhole. She spent hours poring over the data, her mind racing with possibilities.

When she finally presented her findings to Markov, she was met with skepticism. "You're jumping to conclusions," he said. "There's no proof that the energy field is a wormhole."

Sarah refused to back down. She gathered a team of engineers and scientists who shared her passion for exploration and began working on a plan to investigate the wormhole. They faced numerous challenges along the way, including resistance from the council and technical difficulties with the equipment.

But Sarah was undeterred. She poured her heart and soul into the project, determined to uncover the truth about the energy field. And finally, after weeks of hard work and perseverance, they were ready.

As they activated the equipment and opened the wormhole, Sarah felt a surge of adrenaline rush through her body. She watched in awe as the wormhole opened up before her, revealing a dazzling array of stars and galaxies beyond.

"This is it," she whispered to herself. "The edge of eternity."

The team stepped through the wormhole, ready to embark on a journey of discovery that would change the course of human history forever. But as they entered the unknown, Sarah couldn't help but wonder what dangers lay ahead. Would they find new worlds and civilizations, or would they be consumed by the vast emptiness of space?

Only time would tell, but Sarah was ready to face whatever challenges lay in store. She was driven by a fierce curiosity and a desire to push the boundaries of what was possible. And as she took her first steps into the unknown, she felt a sense of exhilaration that she knew would never fade.

CHAPTER THREE

RESISTANCE

The laboratory was bustling with activity as Sarah's team worked to prepare the equipment for the wormhole exploration. The scientists and engineers were giddy with excitement at the prospect of discovering what lay beyond the energy field, but there was an undercurrent of tension in the room.

Markov stood off to the side, his arms folded across his chest, watching the proceedings with a scowl. He had made it clear that he didn't think the wormhole exploration was worth the risk, and he was openly hostile to Sarah and her team.

Sarah tried to ignore Markov's disapproving glare as she conferred with her team. They were discussing the calculations needed to stabilize the wormhole, and Sarah was in her element. She loved the challenge of solving complex problems, especially when it had the potential to change the course of human history.

But as the meeting wore on, Sarah noticed that Markov was becoming increasingly agitated. He interrupted her mid-sentence, his voice laced with anger.

"I've had enough of this nonsense," he said, his eyes blazing. "We're wasting our time and resources on a pipe dream. You're jeopardizing the entire colony with your reckless pursuit of the unknown."

Sarah could feel the tension in the room rising as Markov's outburst reverberated through the laboratory. She knew she needed to remain calm and rational, but she couldn't help feeling angry and frustrated.

"Markov, I understand your concerns, but we can't ignore the potential benefits of exploring the wormhole. It could revolutionize our understanding of the universe and open up new opportunities for the colony."

Markov snorted. "I'll believe it when I see it. You're just chasing after some romanticized notion of discovery, without considering the consequences."

Sarah bristled at the implication that she wasn't thinking through the risks involved. She knew the dangers of exploring the unknown, but she believed that the potential rewards were worth it.

"We've calculated the risks and taken every precaution," she said firmly. "And we have the support of many others in the colony who share our vision. We're not going to let fear hold us back from making history."

Markov scowled, but he didn't respond. Sarah could tell that the argument was far from over, but she hoped that her words had at least made a dent in his skepticism.

As the meeting adjourned and the team began to disperse, Sarah couldn't help feeling a sense of unease. She knew that the road ahead would be fraught with obstacles, and that not everyone in the colony would be on their side. But she was determined to push forward, to explore the wormhole and discover what lay beyond the edge of eternity.

CHAPTER FOUR

OBSTACLES

The work was grueling, and progress was slow. Sarah and her team spent long days preparing the equipment needed to open the wormhole, battling against technical difficulties and sabotage from members of the council who were opposed to the project.

Sarah's mind was consumed by the prospect of discovering what lay on the other side of the energy field, and the thought of failure was unbearable. She pushed her team to their limits, refusing to accept anything less than perfection.

As the days turned into weeks, the team encountered obstacle after obstacle. The equipment needed to be tested and retested, every detail meticulously examined to ensure that it would withstand the tremendous power of the wormhole. They worked in shifts, never sleeping for more than a few hours at a time, their eyes bloodshot and their bodies weary.

But the real challenge came in the form of sabotage. Someone was tampering with the equipment, causing mysterious malfunctions that threatened to derail the entire project. Sarah knew that the council was desperate to stop her, but she never expected the lengths to which they would go.

She worked around the clock, scouring every inch of the equipment for signs of tampering. She even began to suspect members of her own team, wondering if they had been bribed or threatened into betraying her. But no matter how hard she looked, she could never find any concrete evidence.

As the tension mounted, Sarah began to feel her resolve slipping. She had been so consumed by her passion for discovery that she had forgotten the dangers that came with it. The council would stop at nothing to maintain their power, and they saw her as a threat. But she refused to give up. She refused to let them win.

Finally, after weeks of painstaking work, the team was ready to open the wormhole. Sarah's heart was pounding as she watched the final preparations being made. The wormhole generator hummed to life, the air crackling with energy as the machine built up to full power.

For a moment, everything was still. Then, with a blinding flash, the energy field collapsed inward, opening a portal to another dimension.

Sarah felt a surge of exhilaration as she watched the wormhole open. This was it, the moment she had been waiting for. She stepped forward, ready to take the first steps into the unknown.

But as she approached the portal, a figure emerged from the shadows, a council member with a weapon in his hand. He aimed it directly at Sarah, a look of hatred in his eyes.

"You're not going anywhere, Sarah," he snarled. "This ends here."

Sarah stood frozen, her mind racing as she tried to think of a way out of the situation. But before she could react, one of her team members stepped forward, a wrench in his hand.

"I don't think so," he said, swinging the wrench at the council member's head.

The blow connected, and the council member crumpled to the ground, unconscious.

Sarah looked at her team member, a mixture of shock and gratitude on her face. She knew that they had risked everything to make this project a reality. And now, with the wormhole open and the council's power threatened, there was no telling what would happen next.

CHAPTER FIVE

Through the Wormhole

Sarah couldn't believe her eyes as she emerged from the wormhole. She had spent months preparing for this moment, but no amount of preparation could have prepared her for what lay ahead. Before her and her team stretched out a galaxy beyond their wildest dreams. Stars twinkled in the distance, and planets orbited them in intricate patterns.

They were surrounded by a vast expanse of space, a seemingly endless sea of stars and nebulas, but Sarah's attention was immediately drawn to a nearby planet. It looked remarkably like Earth, with blue oceans, green forests, and white clouds, but she knew it couldn't be the same planet. The atmosphere was different, and the continents were shaped differently. It was an entirely different world.

Sarah and her team made contact with the planet's inhabitants, a species that resembled humanoid cats, with sleek fur and expressive eyes. At first, the aliens were wary of the humans, but they soon warmed up to them, fascinated by their advanced technology and their desire to explore new worlds. Sarah and her team spent weeks learning about the planet's ecology and culture, and they were amazed by the level of sophistication and artistry they encountered.

As they explored further, they discovered more and more worlds, each one more wondrous than the last. They visited a planet covered entirely in crystals, where the sun shone through the crystals, casting rainbows on the ground. They traveled to a planet where the oceans glowed with bioluminescent creatures, and the sky was filled with auroras. They even encountered a planet that was home to a species of sentient machines, who welcomed them with open arms and showed them the secrets of their technology.

Sarah and her team were in awe of the vastness of the universe, and the infinite possibilities that lay before them. They had gone from the edge of eternity to the edge of the unknown, and they were determined to explore every last corner of it.

But their euphoria was short-lived. Markov and the council had caught wind of their progress and were growing increasingly alarmed by their lack of communication. They were convinced that Sarah and her team had met with disaster, and they had dispatched a team to bring them back to Eternum by any means necessary.

Sarah and her team knew that they had to act fast if they wanted to avoid capture, and they decided to make a run for it. They gathered up their equipment and raced to the wormhole, hoping to escape before the council's soldiers arrived. But as they reached the entrance to the wormhole, they saw that it was already too late. The soldiers had arrived, and they were blocking their path.

Sarah drew her weapon, knowing that she had to fight for her right to explore the universe. She and her team prepared to make a final stand, ready to face whatever lay ahead. They had come too far to be stopped now.

CHAPTER SIX

CONFRONTATION

Sarah and her team had successfully entered the wormhole and found themselves in a completely different galaxy. They had made contact with an alien civilization and begun to explore new worlds. However, the euphoria of discovery was short-lived. Word of their success had reached Markov and the council on Eternum, and they were not happy.

Sarah was aware that her actions had caused a stir back on Eternum, but she had never imagined that it would come to this. The council had sent a team of soldiers to bring her back, but Sarah and her team were not going to give up without a fight.

The soldiers had arrived in the dead of night, their ships landing with a deafening thud that shook the ground. Sarah and her team had been on high alert since they first heard the ships approaching, and they had been ready for the confrontation that was about to come.

The two sides faced each other across a field of rough terrain, the soldiers' guns drawn and trained on Sarah and her team. Sarah stood tall, her hands held up in surrender, but her eyes never left Markov's.

"You've caused enough trouble, Sarah," Markov said, his voice cold and distant. "It's time to come home."

"I can't do that, Markov," Sarah replied, her voice just as firm. "We've discovered something incredible, something that could change everything."

"You're not thinking clearly, Sarah," Markov said, taking a step forward. "This is dangerous. You have no idea what kind of threats are out there. You're risking our entire colony by pursuing this."

"I know what I'm doing, Markov," Sarah said. "I've got a team of the best scientists and engineers with me. We're prepared for anything that comes our way."

"You're putting too much faith in your team," Markov said, his eyes flashing with anger. "This is a mistake, Sarah. A mistake that could cost us everything."

The tension between the two sides was palpable, and Sarah knew that one wrong move could ignite a war. She took a step forward, her eyes locked on Markov's.

"Let us go, Markov," she said. "Let us finish what we've started. This is bigger than just our colony. This is about the future of our species. Don't stand in our way."

Markov hesitated for a moment, then nodded. "Very well," he said. "You can continue your work. But if you get into any trouble, don't expect us to come to your aid."

Sarah breathed a sigh of relief as the soldiers lowered their weapons and retreated back to their ships. She knew that the battle was far from over, but for now, they had won this round.

As the ships disappeared into the night sky, Sarah turned to her team. "We've got work to do," she said. "Let's finish what we started."

The team looked at each other, their faces determined. They knew that the road ahead would be long and difficult, but they were ready to face whatever challenges lay ahead.

As they resumed their mission, Sarah couldn't help but feel a sense of pride and satisfaction. She was living her dream, exploring the universe and making new discoveries. And she was doing it on her own terms, no matter what the consequences might be.

CHAPTER SEVEN

BETRAYAL

Sarah's heart was pounding as she watched the screen flicker and die. "What happened?" she shouted, turning to face the rest of the team.

The silence that followed was deafening. They all knew what it meant. They were trapped. Stranded in a galaxy far from home with no way to get back.

"We need to fix it," Sarah said, her voice firm despite the panic that was rising in her chest. "We can't give up now."

But as they began to work on the equipment, it quickly became clear that the damage was too severe. Someone had sabotaged the power supply, and it would take days, if not weeks, to repair.

Sarah felt a wave of anger and frustration wash over her. Who would do something like this? Who would betray them at a time like this?

It didn't take long for the team to figure out who was responsible. One of their own, a man they had trusted and relied on, had turned out to be a spy for the council.

Sarah's mind was racing as she tried to process the betrayal. How long had he been working for the council? What other information had he given them? And how were they going to get out of this mess?

As they sat in the dimly-lit chamber, surrounded by the wreckage of their hopes and dreams, Sarah realized that they were on their own. They couldn't rely on anyone else to save them. They had to find a way out themselves.

With a sense of grim determination, Sarah rallied her team. They began to explore the alien world around them, using their scientific knowledge to survive and adapt. They learned from the local inhabitants, forming alliances and building relationships.

But even as they worked to survive, Sarah knew that they had to find a way back to Eternum. The wormhole was their only hope, and it was still open. But they needed power to activate it, and their power supply was destroyed.

Sarah's mind was consumed with finding a solution. She worked tirelessly, poring over schematics and calculations, trying to find a way to get the power they needed.

And then, one day, it clicked. She had found a way to harness the energy of the sun and use it to power their equipment. It was risky and experimental, but it just might work.

With a sense of nervous excitement, Sarah and her team set to work on the new plan. They built the new equipment, tested it, and prepared to make the jump back to Eternum.

As they stood in front of the wormhole, ready to take the leap, Sarah couldn't help but feel a sense of anticipation. They had come so far, and yet the journey was just beginning.

With a deep breath, she gave the order to activate the wormhole. The energy field crackled and shimmered, and then, in a blinding flash, they were gone.

But when they emerged on the other side, they found that things had changed. The council was gone, replaced by a new regime that saw Sarah and her team as a threat. The future was uncertain, but one thing was clear: they had only just begun to scratch the surface of what lay beyond the edge of eternity.

CHAPTER EIGHT

SURVIVAL

The alien world was a hostile and unfamiliar place, but Sarah and her team were determined to survive. They had brought equipment and supplies, but they quickly discovered that many of their assumptions about the environment were wrong.

The atmosphere was thick and humid, making it difficult to breathe. The ground was covered in a thick layer of moss that made it slippery and hard to walk on. The local flora and fauna were unlike anything they had ever seen before, with strange colors and textures that seemed almost alien.

Despite the challenges, Sarah and her team were scientists and engineers, and they were used to problem-solving. They quickly got to work using their knowledge to adapt to the new environment.

They set up a base camp in a small clearing, using their equipment to create shelter and filter the air. They began to explore the surrounding area, taking samples of the plants and animals and analyzing the soil and water.

Sarah was particularly fascinated by the local flora, which seemed to have properties that could be useful in medicine and other fields. She spent hours studying the plants, taking notes and making sketches.

One day, while exploring a nearby cave system, Sarah and her team discovered a strange fungus that glowed in the dark. It had a unique chemical composition that they believed could be used as a power source.

Excited by the possibilities, they began to collect samples of the fungus and experiment with it. They used their equipment to extract the chemicals and test their properties.

As they worked, they began to notice changes in the local ecosystem. Animals that had been scarce or nonexistent began to appear, drawn by the light and energy of the fungus. The surrounding plants also seemed to be growing faster and stronger.

Sarah and her team realized that their actions were having unintended consequences, and they began to reassess their approach. They shifted their focus to understanding the ecosystem as a whole, rather than just exploiting individual components.

Over time, they began to develop a deeper understanding and appreciation for the alien world they had found themselves on. They formed relationships with the local inhabitants, learning their language and customs.

As the weeks turned into months, Sarah and her team realized that they had found something truly remarkable. They had survived in a hostile environment and made groundbreaking discoveries, but they had also learned the value of humility and respect for the natural world.

As they prepared to return to Eternum, they knew that their lives would never be the same. They had crossed the threshold of the known universe and seen things that would change the course of history. And they had done it all by working together, trusting their instincts, and never giving up.

CHAPTER NINE

RETURN

Sarah and her team worked tirelessly to repair the equipment that would allow them to travel back through the wormhole and return to Eternum. They had to be careful, as the council had become increasingly suspicious of Sarah's actions, and she knew that they would not hesitate to stop her if they discovered what she was doing.

Despite the challenges, Sarah and her team finally managed to repair the equipment and initiate the return sequence. The energy field flickered and crackled, and for a moment, it seemed as though the wormhole would collapse under the strain. But then, with a sudden burst of energy, the wormhole stabilized, and Sarah and her team were able to step through and return to Eternum.

As they emerged on the other side, Sarah could see that things had changed. The council had been replaced by a more authoritarian regime, one that saw Sarah as a threat to their power. She could see armed soldiers lining the walls of the colony, their weapons trained on her and her team.

"Step forward, Dr. Williams," a voice boomed over the intercom. "You have been accused of treason against the colony. Surrender now, and you will be given a fair trial."

Sarah hesitated, uncertain of what to do. She knew that if she surrendered, she would be putting her life in the hands of the new council, and she wasn't sure she could trust them. But at the same time, she couldn't fight her way out of this situation on her own.

She turned to her team, seeking their advice.

"We'll back you up, Sarah," one of her team members said, his hand resting on his weapon. "Whatever you decide, we're with you."

Sarah took a deep breath, steeling herself for what was to come. She stepped forward, her hands raised in surrender, and waited as the soldiers closed in around her.

But then, to her surprise, something unexpected happened. A group of citizens, who had grown disillusioned with the council's authoritarian tactics, emerged from the shadows and began to protest. They shouted slogans, demanding that Sarah be given a fair trial and that the council's actions be questioned.

The soldiers hesitated, uncertain of what to do. The protest grew louder, and Sarah realized that she might have a chance after all. She began to speak, addressing the crowd and calling for unity against the oppressive council. Her words struck a chord with the citizens, and they rallied behind her, forming a human shield between her and the soldiers.

In that moment, Sarah realized that her journey had not just been about exploration and discovery, but about the power of hope and the importance of standing up for what was right. She had discovered a new world, but she had also rediscovered the power of the human spirit, and the fact that even in the darkest of times, there was always hope.

CHAPTER TEN

EPILOGUE

Sarah stood at the edge of the colony, looking out at the vast expanse of space. She had made her decision: it was time to leave Eternum behind and continue exploring the galaxy. As she turned to walk away, Markov approached her.

"I'm sorry, Sarah," he said, his voice heavy with regret. "I should have listened to you from the beginning. You were right about the wormhole, and I was wrong to stand in your way."

Sarah paused and looked at Markov, studying him for a moment. She could see the sincerity in his eyes, and she knew that he meant what he said.

"It's not too late, Markov," she said, her tone softening. "We can still work together to make things right."

But Markov shook his head. "No, Sarah. It's too late for me. I've made too many mistakes, and I've lost the trust of the people. It's time for me to step down and let someone else take the reins."

Sarah nodded, understanding the weight of Markov's decision. "I wish you the best, Markov. And I hope that one day we can work together again."

Markov smiled, his face lined with regret. "I hope so too, Sarah."

As Sarah made her way back to the lab, she felt a sense of relief wash over her. She knew that leaving Eternum behind was the right decision. She was tired of the politics and the petty squabbles of the council. She wanted to explore the universe, to discover new worlds and new civilizations. And she knew that she could do it, with or without the support of the council.

When she reached the lab, she found her team waiting for her. They had packed their bags and were ready to leave Eternum behind.

"Are you sure about this, Sarah?" one of her team members asked, his voice filled with uncertainty.

Sarah smiled. "I've never been more sure of anything in my life."

Together, they made their way to the wormhole, ready to take the leap into the unknown. As they stepped through the energy field, Sarah felt a sense of exhilaration. She knew that they were taking a risk, but she also knew that it was worth it. The universe was waiting for them, and they were ready to explore it.

www.ingramcontent.com/pod-product-compliance
Lightning Source LLC
Chambersburg PA
CBHW030239150726

47988CB00021B/3333